# Kye
# and the
# Cephalopod©

By - Nadia T. Meyers

# KYE AND THE CEPHALOPOD

Written and Illustrated by
Nadia T. Meyers

Published by:  Healing H2Os, LLC

ISBN - 978-1-7348110-2-5

ISBN - 978-1-7348110-1-8

ISBN – 978-1-7348110-0-1

https://healingh2osllc-art.abmp.com/home


eBook created in the United States of America


Library of Congress Control Number: 2020905589

# DEDICATION

To my son Kye DeVonte' White. My first born and inspiration for this literary work. If you keep shooting for your dreams, you're bound to SCORE!

I give thanks and gratitude to my Divine Ancestors YEMAYA and OSHUN for their guidance and wisdom supporting me on my Divine Path.

I AM A WELL-BEHAVED BLACK WOMAN MAKING HISTORY ON MY OWN TERMS WITH ALL THE FREEDOMS AND SOVEREIGNTIES GRANTED TO ME BY MY BIRTHRIGHT!

 - Nadia Meyers

We will no longer be "HIDDEN FIGURES" in the background...We UNAPOLOGETICALLY STEP BOLDLY INTO THE FOREFRONT AND CLAIM WHAT IS OWED TO US! – Nadia Meyers


Rest in Greatness NIPSEY HUSSLE! Your business sense REMAINS A TRUE INSPIRATION FOR THE WORLD! May the Marathon CONTINUE!

STOP POLLUTION! SAVE OUR OCEANS! LEAVE OUR CHILDREN A LEGACY TO BE PROUD OF!


For all those marine scientists who also enjoyed art class...

THIS IS FOR YOU!

# KYE AND THE CEPHALOPOD

*Kye loved the beach.*

*He loved how the sand felt between his toes and how the seashells tasted. He especially loved to run with the water as it washed back and forth along the shore. But what he loved most was all the cool things his Mommie would teach him about the sea.*

1

Although Kye loved the beach and its shores there was something that kept him from going out in the sea…The Cephalopod!

The cephalopod was a sea creature that had a huge head, no body, two enormous eyes, and lots of arms…eight in some cases. It crept along the seafloor looking in cracks and over nooks for food.

"So, watch where you sit…because the cephalopod is gonna get you!" Kye's Mommie would say just before she'd tickle him.

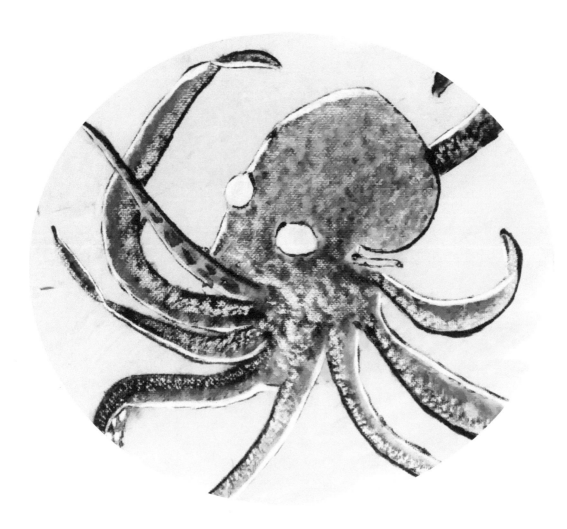

She always meant it as a joke but Kye took her words very seriously. He soon became uneasy around any body of water where he could not see clear to the bottom.

When Kye went fishing, he'd never dangle his feet over the pond. He quit taking baths because once his water got dirty, he could not see the basin floor. And he was absolutely afraid to use the potty because it connected to a pipe that stretched all the way to the sea.

Kye was very disturbed by the cephalopod. He really thought that it was gonna get him!

One day while fishing, Kye's hook caught hold of something.

"I got a fish!" he yelled excitingly to his Mommie.

As Kye reeled up the fish his Mommie ran to get their bucket. All of a sudden, a huge arm came up out of the pond and snatched the fish right off Kye's hook. Two enormous eyes glared from the most gigantic head Kye had ever seen.

"I'm gonna get you!" the cephalopod said then quickly sunk back into the pond.

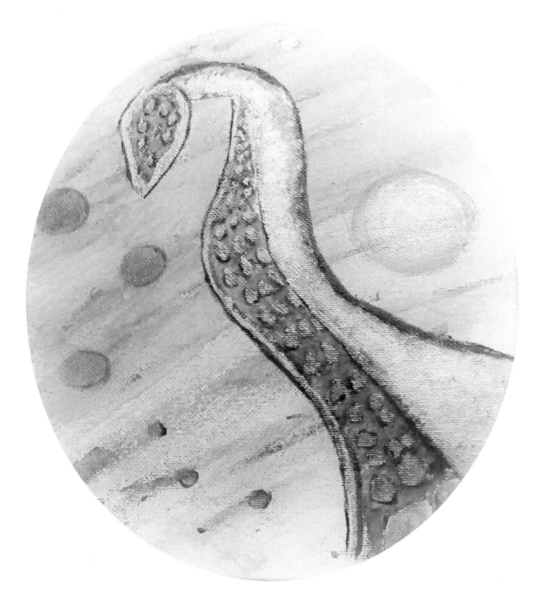

When Kye's Mommie returned she looked around and asked Kye, "Where's the fish?"  Kye stuttered, "T-the cephalopod took it!"

"Impossible…" Kye's Mommie said. "Cephalopods only live in the sea!" she laughed.

"But Mommie, it said its gonna get me!" he cried.

Kye's Mommie thought maybe Kye received too much sun for the day and decided that it was time to go home.

At home, his Mommie ran some warm water for his bath.  She sang songs, read stories, and told jokes to Kye and he soon became wrinkled from being in the tub.  He also forgot all about the cephalopod.  After Kye had been bathed, his Mommie remembered she left his towel in the laundry basket in the next room.

"I forgot your towel, sweetie…I'll be right back."

As soon as she passed through the door, two arms came out of the water and snatched Kye's soap and wash cloth.  Once again, the two enormous eyes and gigantic head arose.

The cephalopod said, "Kye, I'm gonna get you!"

Kye screamed and quickly jumped out of the tub, just as his Mommie was coming back in.

She wrapped him oh so tightly in the towel and asked him, "Why did you scream like so?" She was very concerned.

Kye shook in her arms as she warmed him by rubbing his back over the towel.

"The cephalopod came and grabbed the soap and cloth and said he was gonna get me!" He hurried.

Kye's Mommie spoke in her most soothing voice, "Kye, for the last time, cephalopods live in the sea, not in our bathtub."

Kye's Mommie decided she had to find the happiest stories to read, sing the most happiest of songs, and tell the most funniest of jokes to get his mind off this cephalopod nonsense.

And that's just what she did. Kye laughed so hard at the jokes, his sides hurt. He sang so loud; he lost his voice. The stories were so amazing that he quickly drifted into a deep sleep, dreaming of faraway lands. Kye had completely forgotten about the cephalopod.

"Clink"

Kye sat up.

"Thump"

Kye wiped his eyes.

"What was that?" he thought.

 He got up and went to the bathroom.

    "Clunk, clunk, clunk", sounded just as he flicked on the light. "I said I was gonna get you!" Kye heard, as he stared into those two enormous eyes with the gigantic head.  This time he counted eight arms as the cephalopod climbed out of the potty.

"Mommie!" he tried to scream, but his voice was still lost from the happy songs he sang.

The cephalopod grabbed him and carried him back to the potty. Kye tried to wiggle himself loose from the cephalopods grip, but his sides still hurt from all his laughing. As the cephalopod began climbing into the potty, all Kye could think of was the faraway lands this creature would probably take him where he would never see his Mommie again.

Kye grew very angry with the cephalopod.

"You are NOT taking ME from MY Mommie!" He thought.

The cephalopod had gotten completely in the potty except for the arm that held Kye over the hole. Just as the arm began to back Kye through, he said to himself, "Here's my chance."

His courage increased and his heart began to race and Kye did the most unthinkable thing he could imagine.

He used the potty!

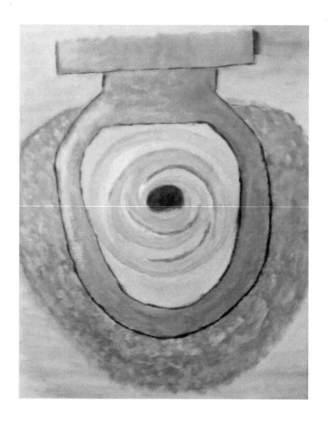

The cephalopod quickly went down the potty. "And stay out!"

Kye shouted as he flushed the potty, surprised by the return of his voice.  Just then Kye's Mommie stood at the door.

"Kye, who are you talking to and why are you up so late?"

"I had to use the potty," He giggled and glanced at the potty.

His Mommie picked him up.

"Are you sure? Because I thought you would say…that the cephalopod was trying to get you!" she joked and began tickling him.

As she put Kye to bed she looked in his eyes.

"I love you so much, son." She said.

*Kye still loves the beach.*

*He still likes how the sand feels between his toes and how the shells taste. Running along the shore is still fun. Kye even found that going into the water isn't half bad, now that he knows how to defeat the cephalopod. But what Kye loved most of all is his Mommie.*

# THE END...

# ... OR IS IT???

# cephalopod

[ **sef**-*uh*-l*uh*-pod ]

*noun*

any mollusk of the class Cephalopoda, having tentacles attached to the head, including the cuttlefish, squid, and octopus.

*adjective*

Also, **ceph·a·lo·pod·ic, ceph·a·lop·o·dous** [sef-*uh*-**lop**-*uh*-d*uh* s] . belonging or pertaining to the Cephalopoda.

For more information on octopuses and ocean literacy click the links below.

http://www.dnr.sc.gov/marine/sertc/Featured%20Species%20O%20vulgaris.pdf

http://oceanliteracy.wp2.coexploration.org/

Nadia T. Meyers earned her Bachelor of Science (Marine Option) from Millersville University, Millersville, Pennsylvania, USA, where she was the first African American to graduate from the marine biology program, in 2001.

In 2010, she also became the first African American to gain a Master of Marine Science in Marine Policy from Savannah State University, Savannah, Georgia, USA, producing a pilot study social science thesis addressing how to effectively matriculate more people of color (POC) into marine science careers.

She has maintained marine invertebrate taxonomic employments as a Wildlife Biologist with South Carolina Department of Natural Resources (SCDNR), Southeastern Regional Taxonomic Center (SERTC), and as a Benthic Research Lab Technician at Savannah State University (SSU).

Nadia's love for cephalopods stemmed from her undergraduate independent research on the spatial learning of octopuses by placing them in mazes to explore if octopuses utilize landscape cues to identify their dens.

Currently, Nadia is an entrepreneur/author/painter/artist merging her passions with marine science which led her to present different projects at global marine science conferences hosted by Massachusetts Institute of Technology (MIT) and Association for the Sciences of Limnology and Oceanography (ASLO).

In a nutshell…she's pretty cool peeps!

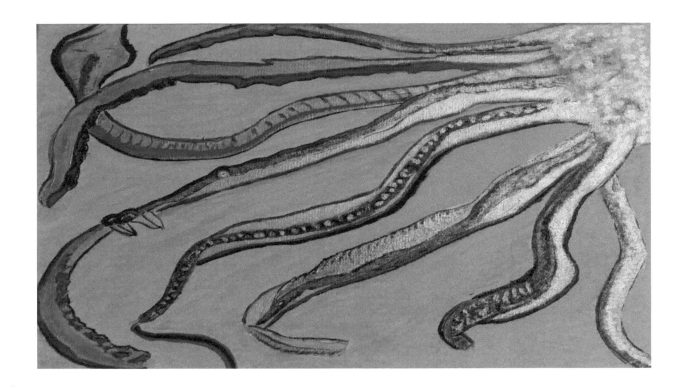

"Kye and the Cephalopod" is a tale of a boy who loves the seashores but has a scary fear of what lies beneath. By overcoming his fear, he gains confidence to enter the sea. This book provides children an early introduction to one of the most villainous creatures of the sea and focuses on facing one's fear "in thought" can lead to produce positive exposures in one's "reality."

$22.00
ISBN 978-1-7348110-0-1
52200>

9 781734 811001

CPSIA information can be obtained
at www.ICGtesting.com
Printed in the USA
LVHW071345110620
657867LV00036B/2079

* 9 7 8 1 7 3 4 8 1 1 0 0 1 *